ghosts of christmas presents

A GHOST WRITING HOLIDAY NOVELLA

DANIELLE SMYTH

ASTRALUMEN PRESS

This is a work of fiction. Names, characters, businesses, places, events, and incidents are either the products of the author's imagination or used in a fictitious manner. Any resemblance to actual persons, living or dead, or actual events is purely coincidental.

Book cover design by Danielle Smyth.

Editing by Dan Smyth.

ISBN (Paperback): 979-8-9933163-4-5 | ISBN (Hardcover): 979-8-9933163-5-2 | ISBN (Kindle eBook): 979-8-9933163-3-8

Library of Congress Control Number: PENDING

Publisher's Cataloging-in-Publication data

Smyth, Danielle, author.

Ghosts of Christmas Presents: A Ghost Writing Novella / Danielle Smyth. — First edition. — Burnt Hills, NY: Astralumen Press, 2025.

Edited by Dan Smyth; cover design and illustration by Danielle Smyth.

LCCN: 2025949692

ISBN (Paperback): 979-8-9933163-4-5 | ISBN (Hardcover): 979-8-9933163-5-2 | ISBN (Kindle eBook): 979-8-9933163-3-8

LCSH: Christmas stories—Fiction | Romance fiction | Contemporary romance fiction | Holiday fiction | Couples—Fiction

Classification: LCC: PS3619.M66 G47 2025 | DDC: 813/.6–dc23

Visit the author's website at www.daniellesmythbooks.com

Printed in the U.S.A.

Published by Astralumen Press: www.astralumenpress.com

To L+D, for making the holidays magical

Christmas hits differently when you're an adult. No longer is it a delightful whirlwind of sensory overload; of bright colors, twinkling lights, sweet treats, and crinkly paper. As you shed the whimsical mantle of childhood and reluctantly assume the dull business casual required of grown-ups, some of the magic disappears.

It's not always obvious exactly when it happens, or how. But gradually, the things that used to seem miraculous—so exciting that your little brain could barely handle them—become just sentimental holdovers from the before times. The times when someone else was responsible for making the holidays magical *for* you. Without you even realizing until it's too late, Christmas morphs into a vaguely melancholy, often quite stressful, day of familial obligation.

I'm trying so, so hard not to let that happen this year.

I wake up on Christmas Eve to the sound of my phone buzzing on my nightstand. Rolling over with a groan, I grab it and blearily crack open one eye. It's my mother.

I try to answer, but I don't quite get there before the call ends. Fortunately, she dials me back immediately.

"Hello?" I whisper, trying to walk the line between being too quiet that she can't hear me and being so loud that I wake up Will, who's sleeping peacefully beside me.

"Callie, it's your mother."

"Yes, I know, Mom. Cell phones have this magical thing called caller ID. In fact, they have for some time now."

I know phone signals have to bounce all the way to a cell tower and back down, but even with that separation between us, I'm pretty sure I can hear her sigh deeply before she even does so.

Will and I like to joke that my mom, who is without question a brilliant woman, has started suffering in the last year or so from a condition we've christened "EOE"—Early-Onset Esperanza. Though she's still just as sharp as ever, she sometimes says and does things that leave us scratching our heads. Like calling twice in a row and then identifying herself when I answer.

That's such an Esperanza move.

"Anyway. We wanted to talk to you about tomorrow."

My heart starts racing in my chest. My parents are supposed to come for Christmas dinner at Will's and my apartment tomorrow evening. It's our first holiday season together in this cozy two-bedroom, just three blocks away from the library, and we've never hosted a party here. I'd be lying if I said I didn't want to show it off, all decked out in its festive trimmings.

I hope nothing has derailed my parents' plans.

"Okay. What about it?" I sit up in bed, accidentally knocking into Will's forearm. He starts to stir, smiling up at me sleepily.

I mute myself and give him a quick kiss on the cheek.

"We're still coming, but we were curious if you'd be open to a couple more guests."

The silence on the line feels deafening, because I already know what she's going to say next. Or at least who it is she's talking about. And I'm not all that eager to hear it.

"Your grandparents had Christmas plans with Melanie, but those fell through. Mel's got some sort of fight going on with Rob about who gets the kids for the holidays, and she's going to have to set up shop in a hotel outside Philadelphia in order to see them on Christmas."

"Geez, you'd think a lawyer would be a little better at ensuring she gets Christmas with her kids," I joke, pulling my favorite pink fleece blanket more tightly around my chest.

Will and I were up late last night watching *Die Hard*, which holds a special spot in our hearts given the role it played in getting us together in the first place. Plus, Will insists it's the greatest Christmas movie of all time. (My vote goes to *The Muppet Christmas Carol*, but why quibble.) Afterward, we got a little distracted with each other, and I forgot to get dressed before I fell asleep. In any case, it's pretty chilly in our room this morning.

Will rubs his arm up and down my back when he sees me shrinking into the warmth of the blanket. "Thank you," I mouth to him.

"Yeah, well, Melanie couldn't close the deal this time," Mom goes on. "So now your grandparents don't have anywhere to go for dinner tomorrow. I'm happy to shift the party to our house, and of course, Molly and your friends would be welcome, too, but I know how excited you were to host everyone."

I nod slowly. Things have been a little weird with my grandparents ever since Esperanza died almost a year and a half ago. Outwardly, there's no conflict, and my conversation with my grandmother after the funeral left our relationship in a good place.

But internally, I'm still grappling with the loss of Esperanza, which feels like it should have been wholly preventable, and the role my grandmother played in derailing Esperanza's chance at a happy ending with Johnny, the man she never stopped loving.

Don't even get me started on my feelings towards my other great-aunt, Maria, whom I can't help but blame for Esperanza's death.

I've worked hard to walk the path toward forgiveness, especially since I know it's what Esperanza would want. I've even started seeing a therapist, because I know I need a little more help dealing with my grief and the complicated emotions that come along with it.

But I haven't gone out of my way to spend time with my grandparents since Esperanza died. I've seen them from time to time, but only when someone else arranged it. Things are a little too weird, and raw, and, anyway, Esperanza was the glue that held us together. Without her around, Josephine and I have very little to discuss.

My grandfather and I never talked, period, because he was typically too busy nodding off in his rocking chair or complaining to my dad about the stock market to pay me any mind.

But it's Christmas, and we've got ingredients for about 15 different appetizers and side dishes already waiting in the refrigerator. I know we have enough food.

And then there's the perfect little tree that Will patiently sawed down from a farm out near Rockledge, while I stood by and shouted inane instructions to him like, "Saw it harder that way," and "No, your other left," until the Douglas fir finally flopped over onto the ground.

We'd decorated it within an inch of its life with everything from garland to shells we got on this year's summer beach vacation. We even added a miniature version of Will's book, *Fault Lines*, which I made him out of clay for his last birthday.

I don't know if it's the loss of Esperanza, or the slightly hollow feeling that tends to crop up around Christmas ever since I became an adult, but I'm desperate for the holidays to be full of warmth and light and meaning again. Things have been feeling very warm and cozy and wonderful, in general, ever since Will and I started dating two summers ago, but I still have an urge to gather our families and friends together to bring back some semblance of the holiday magic I used to love when I was a kid.

I wonder what my therapist would have to say about that. I could probably give her a full day's worth of things to psychoanalyze about my stunted development as an adult. I make a mental note to share some of these thoughts with her the next time we meet.

To my mother, all I say is, "Yes, of course they can come. Do you want to call them, or should I?"

"I'll call your grandmother now. Thanks, Callie. I appreciate it." Mom sounds relieved, like she wasn't entirely sure I was going to say yes. That makes me a little sad, honestly.

"Sounds good. Tell them not to worry about bringing anything, please. We have more than enough food."

"Will do. See you tomorrow, okay? Enjoy your Christmas Eve!"

"You too. Love you!"

"Love you, too, honey."

Will rolls over with a raised brow and a grin on his face. "So I take it we need to grab those extra folding chairs that Susan offered us?"

I chuckle. "I guess we do. Is it cool with you if my grandparents come tomorrow?"

"Hey, as long as you're fine with it," Will says, wrapping his arms around me and pulling me back down next to him, "there's always room at the inn."

two

When Will and I finally make it out of the bedroom at 11:30, I fire off a quick text to Susan, asking if we can borrow her chairs. She and Doug and their kids are joining us for the holiday tomorrow, because her parents are out of town, fulfilling a lifelong dream to tour London at Christmastime. She'd wanted to go along with them, but ultimately decided she needed to wait until Freya was a bit older. "I can't imagine dragging a kindergartener around Westminster Abbey," she'd told me ruefully.

Will and I were quick to invite Susan and her family to our place. They don't have anyone else in the area, and God knows she and Doug could use a break from cooking. To hear Susan talk, it's more or less all she does when she's not at work.

Plus, it's always fun to play with her kids. And to shop for them. Will and I spent a glorious afternoon last month wandering the toy aisles of Target. We accumulated approximately 600 gifts for each of Susan and Doug's kids before we regained our self-control and put most of them back.

Still, I'm extremely excited to give Freya, Max, and Josie the two gifts we finally settled on for each of them. Especially Freya. She loves that Will and I are both writers, and we found her a little type-writer that really works. I know she's going to love it.

I'm planning to set it up for her after she opens it. Will keeps teasing me, but I couldn't care less—I'm pretty eager to play with it, too.

Scarlett and Jonathan are coming over, also. Jonathan's family is Jewish, so he doesn't need to worry about missing out on Christmas with them. And ever since Jonathan proposed, Scarlett will go liter-ally anywhere as long as he's invited, too. Okay, that might also have been true before their engagement. In any case, she said her parents were fine with her missing their holiday gathering as long as she came home for New Year's.

Scarlett's going to bring spinach dip, which I'm more than a little excited about. She isn't always great at following recipes, mostly because she's so easily distracted, but Jonathan is a great influence on her. I trust him to actually read the ingredient list *before* starting to cook.

How many chairs do you need? Susan texts me back almost imme-diately.

I do a quick count. My parents, Will and I, Scarlett and Jonathan, Will's sister Molly, and Susan and her family make twelve. With the addition of my grandparents, we'll have fourteen. We have six chairs at Esperanza's old dining table, plus two desk chairs and four folding chairs of our own.

Only two. Thank you!

"Hey, did we remember to grab champagne?" Will is sticking his head in the refrigerator, moving containers around.

"I don't think so. But we have wine. We don't need both, right? At least, not until New Year's Eve."

He's still half-buried in our LG. "I'll grab some later. For mimosas."

I don't see why we need mimosas tomorrow, but I decide to let it go. I have other things on my mind.

"I'm going to check my email really quickly," I tell him. "I'll be right back."

Will emerges from the fridge and grins, eyes twinkling. "Callie. It's Christmas Eve. I don't think you're going to be hearing from Jess today."

I wrinkle my nose at him. "I'm just going to check anyway."

Ever since I submitted my Esperanza manuscript to Jess, my agent, she's been presenting it to her contacts at various publishing houses. I decided to call it *Ghost Writing*, because I felt that title perfectly encapsulated what I was doing: writing a story on behalf of the ghosts who could no longer speak for themselves.

In any case, there haven't been any bites yet, but I know Jess had a few meetings last week. I've been refreshing my inbox to a degree my therapist has called "obsessive," but I can't help it. This is a big deal for me.

I'd honestly expected my first manuscript, the one that Will beta-read for me in the library way back when, to be the first one to sell. And I gave it to Jess right away, but I was also working on *Ghost Writing* at the same time.

"Let's wait until you've finished the second one," she'd said. "Then, we can pitch whichever one is strongest. Alternatively, we can pitch both. Either way, I'll have two at my disposal when I'm talking to publishing reps."

Fortunately, it only took me three months to finish *Ghost Writing*. Perhaps because it's about Esperanza, I found it very easy to write. The words just flowed from me like they'd been written on my heart all along.

Jess had been super impressed by both manuscripts, and she's been actively peddling both to the publishing houses she meets with. "It's only a matter of time," she keeps telling me.

Easy for her to say. These are just my hopes and dreams, bound up in paper and ink.

I'd also counted on these books being a source of income. Maybe not a major one; Scarlett and Will have told me plenty about how little authors really earn in royalties. But still, *some* money for all of my hard work would be nice. Since the publishing process is dragging on longer than I would have liked, I've taken on various side projects in the interim.

I've actually started co-teaching a writing class at the library with Lilly, Will's college advisor, which has been beyond wonderful. And while I don't think I'll return to marketing copywriting anytime soon, I've found some other freelance projects that feel particularly meaningful, just to fill in the gaps.

My work for a local literacy nonprofit has been hugely fulfilling, and I'm going to be managing their outreach for next year's Chapters for Change gala. It's enough to pay my bills, and I'm definitely enjoying it.

Besides, Will earns enough at the library to more than cover rent for our tiny apartment. Between his salary and what I'm able to cobble together from my hodge-podge of author-adjacent jobs, we're doing just fine.

Not to mention, Will has done a few book signings for *Fault Lines* since he started back in therapy. He decided it would be therapeutic for him to revisit marketing his novel, since it had meant so much to him.

He's managed to sell a few hundred copies that way over the last year or so. We even got to take a "business trip" up to Maine when he did an author event on the coast. So that's been amazing, too.

Still, I'd really love to see my own publication dreams realized sooner rather than later.

Logging in to see whether today will be the day I receive external validation for my writing is much more of a production than it needs to be, since I have to wait for my laptop to boot up. I know I *could* put my email on my phone, but it stresses me out to see the angry red bubble showing how many unread messages I have. So I exclusively check email on my laptop.

As I key in my password, Will yells in from the kitchen. "Want some breakfast?"

"Sure," I shout back.

"Omelets?"

"You know me so well, babe."

God, how did I get so lucky? Life has defied my wildest expectations ever since Will and I got together. He's reliable, and funny, and supportive, and just...everything. Everything I've ever wanted. Including the world's best omelet chef.

When we first started dating, we spent basically every waking, non-working minute together. Things got a little busier once he started his library science program at Briarford University, but I always made sure to time my writing during his shifts at the library or one of his night classes. That way, we could maximize our time taking walks, cuddling up and reading together, or going to trivia nights.

We split our time between our apartments, at first. But little by little, our belongings started to make their way from one residence to the other. I found myself misplacing at least one outfit per week, and Will lost several books in the cushions of my couch.

One night, it all came to a head when we realized that he'd left his toothbrush at my place, and I'd left mine at his. The situation seemed even funnier than it should have been, because it was two in the morning and we were beyond punch-drunk when we noticed.

"This is very silly," he'd said, gathering me against his chest in front of my bathroom mirror.

"We are beyond help," I'd responded.

"I can think of one way to remedy this." Will had smoothed my hair off my forehead and kissed me gently.

"Oh?"

He'd nodded. "I think we should move in together."

My grin was immediate. "Yes. One hundred times, yes."

Will looked happier than I'd ever seen him. "We'll never lose track of our toothbrushes again."

That night, we shared one toothbrush (his) and fell asleep on the couch, both too caught up in the books we were reading to bother getting ready for bed.

I know it won't always be like this, but honestly, things have been amazing ever since.

My email refreshes and reveals three last-minute holiday shopping ads from Amazon and a credit card statement, but nothing from Jess. Disappointment simmers in my belly, but I try not to fixate on it. There's so much to look forward to over the holidays.

I peek over my shoulder. It looks like Will is sufficiently distracted making the omelets, so I sneak the closet door open and grab my purple backpack, which I'd shoved in the back corner.

Unzipping the top as quietly as I can, I pull a book wrapped in tissue paper from the bottom of the bag. It's a replica of the Book of Kells, and slipped inside the front cover are two plane tickets to Dublin.

Will's been talking for ages about going to Ireland together, in no small part because he's always wanted to visit the Long Room at Trinity College Dublin. It might be one of the most magical libraries ever (other than the one from *Beauty and the Beast*, of course), so it's no wonder he's been practically drooling over the notion of seeing it in person.

To make it even more appealing, Trinity College Dublin is also home to the *real* Book of Kells, a ninth-century illuminated manuscript that is one of Ireland's greatest cultural treasures. It features intricate artwork that reveals a great deal about Irish Christianity and medieval artistry. Not to mention, it's breathtakingly beautiful.

We're going for ten days. We'll start in Dublin and see the Book of Kells and the Long Room. Maybe take a stroll through St. Stephen's Green and tour the Guinness Storehouse. Then, we'll rent a car and head to Kilkenny, Cork, and Waterford. There are castles and monastic ruins and crystal factory tours on my itinerary, plus plenty of Irish stew and Jameson. I've got a stellar lineup of bed-and-breakfasts that came highly rated, both online and from our friend Jenna, who's been to Ireland to visit family several times.

After Waterford, we'll hit up Killarney and make our way to the Ring of Kerry, where I plan to take about three thousand photos. Then, it'll be on to Limerick, and through a series of adorable towns in the countryside en route back to Dublin. I assume, by the time we reach the capital, we'll be exhausted and also heartbroken to be leaving. And, though I've been secretly saving for a year, we'll probably be broke.

It was no small feat, planning an international vacation without Will knowing. Fortunately, in the last year and a half, I've gotten to know his boss pretty well, and she agreed to set aside the vacation time he'd need. I researched bed and breakfasts when Will was at work, and I made all of the reservations on a credit card we don't share. (Our finances have kind of become a jumble of ownership since we moved in together, but we're both okay with it. It does make it hard to plan expensive surprises, though.)

I drag a roll of wrapping paper out from under our bed and lay the book on top of the unfurled edge. I keep scissors and tape in my desk, which is on the other side of the room. If Will keeps cooking, I should be able to sneak past the doorway and grab what I need without him noticing.

"Cal?" Will's footsteps are coming my way. Damn it. *Damn it!* I hastily shove the gift into the backpack and lean over it awkwardly so he can't see what's inside.

"Don't come in here!" I demand, but by the shadow that's fallen across the floor, I can tell it's already too late.

"I'm so sorry," he says, making a big show of shielding his eyes. "Were you wrapping my truckload of presents?"

Snorting, I turn to face him. "That's right. All 20 cubic yards of them."

He laughs. "Sorry. I just wanted to know if you'd prefer cheddar or asiago in your omelet."

"Asiago, obviously."

"That's what I thought."

I grin. "Thank you."

"I'll let you get back to it, then. But the food's basically ready, so maybe save some of this insurmountable wrapping job for later."

I wait until his footsteps recede to take the book back out and begin cutting a piece of sparkly red paper to fit. I can't wait to see his face when he opens this present.

three

After breakfast, we get to work doing food prep for the party tomorrow.

"How am I going to make this cake?" I'm standing over a recipe for a Bûche de Noël, a hugely complicated but gorgeous French dessert that's supposed to look like a tiny yule log.

"I usually recommend following the recipe," Will jokes.

I frown at him. "Very funny. It's just that, when I found this recipe back in October, it somehow seemed very accessible to me as an amateur pastry chef. And now, especially in light of everything else we need to get ready, I'm wondering how I'm going to manage it."

Will leans over my shoulder, his wavy hair brushing against my cheek. "Hmm," he says, reading down the ingredient list. "Do we already have everything we need for this?"

"Yeah. I even got a special pan."

I can feel his eyelashes on my skin. "Couldn't we also just make a normal chocolate cake with what this calls for?"

He's a genius, I'm pretty sure. "I suppose we could do that, yes."

Will steps back and smiles. "Just write 'Happy Birthday Jesus' on top, and it'll still be on-theme."

I swat at him with a dish towel. "You're ridiculous. I'm not sure how well that would go over with my intensely Catholic grandparents."

When my cousin Clare loudly announced that she was an atheist at a family party, I remember how my grandmother quickly crossed herself, then told Clare, "I'll pray that you don't go to the devil."

I suppose the birthday cake idea isn't more egregious than *that*.

"Good point," Will muses, refilling his coffee mug. "Maybe just some festive sprinkles, then?"

"I like that plan." I grab my phone and google chocolate cake recipes.

Will has all the ingredients for Parker House rolls spread out on the opposite counter. He bends over the cookbook across from me on the island, and I lose myself in staring at how his downturned lashes contrast against his skin. How his black hair waves and curls over the top of his head. My fingers inch forward as if of their own volition, practically begging me to explore it.

"I'm going to check the mail real quick," he says suddenly, forcing me out of my daydreams. He sets the cookbook next to his *mise en place* and starts walking toward the door.

I must look confused, because he turns around and adds, "Just while the oven gets to temperature."

I'm not entirely sure how that makes sense, because he'd need to prepare the dough before he could put it into a hot oven, but I nod. "Okay, sounds good."

A solid three minutes of me whisking wet ingredients go by before it occurs to me that the rolls probably need a different baking temperature than the cake. I cross to the opposite counter to check the cookbook, and something catches my eye out the window above the sink.

There's Will, wandering around the parking lot of our apartment complex, snow falling onto the shoulders of his open wool coat. He's talking on the phone, and he looks more than a little annoyed.

He's nowhere near our mailbox.

An uncomfortable sensation bubbles inside me. Will and I have gotten a lot better about conveying our feelings, ever since we almost lost each other due to a failure to communicate. I'm sure both of us being in therapy has helped hugely, but we also make time every week to unload anything that's been weighing on us. Honestly, we've never been so in sync.

But as I watch him pacing around in front of his car, gesticulating a little too wildly for a calm conversation, I can't help but feel concerned. *What is Will keeping from me?*

A few minutes later, the jingle bells on our door announce his return. I try to act like it's reasonable for a trip to the mailbox to take ten minutes, like I didn't notice that he was on the phone.

"Anything good in the mail today?" I attempt to remove all inflection from my voice.

He shakes his head. "Not a thing."

"Almost makes you wish they'd give the postal workers Christmas Eve off, huh?" I smile ruefully. I've never understood why so many businesses stay open the day before Christmas. I realize there are plenty of folks who don't celebrate the holiday, but it feels like we as a society could collectively agree to just *chill* for a day. I mean, if France can manage eight whole weeks of *les grand vacances* every summer, I think our capitalist hellhole should be able to handle two consecutive days.

"I know, right?" Will washes his hands and starts simmering milk for the rolls.

I almost ask him. I really do. But it's Christmas Eve, and I know there can be gift-related secrets even the most honest couples need to keep this time of year. Plus, I've learned, in my time with Will, to let him bring information to me when he's ready to share it. Pushing him before he's prepared to open up never goes well.

So I talk about something else. "Speaking of hardworking civil servants, any word on Lisa's leave next summer?"

Lisa is Will's boss at the library. She's going to be taking a leave of absence for three months next summer to attend her daughter's wedding in London and then travel Europe with her husband. It's a major bucket list item for them, and Will has been coming home almost nightly with tidbits that Lisa's shared about the amazing places she's planning to go.

The way his eyes light up every time he lives vicariously through his colleague's vacation plans is part of the reason I know the Ireland trip will be the perfect Christmas gift.

It's been a bit of a mess at the library, trying to figure out who will serve as interim director next summer. Technically, you need a Master's in Library Science to do it, but they're considering Will for the role. For one thing, they don't have any other easy options. Most of the staff at the library are women who need something to do during the day while their retired husbands "putter" around the garage.

There's also the fact that, after finishing up his BA in the same subject last year, Will enrolled in a Master's program for Library Science at Briarford University. The library board has made it clear, if he sticks around, he'll probably be a shoo-in for Lisa's job when she retires. But she's only 55, so it may be a little bit.

Still, her leave would be an excellent time for him to try his hand at the job, and also to show the library board that he can handle it. I might be even more excited about it than he is, but it's hard not to be thrilled when the person you love most in the world has the opportunity they've always wanted.

Will and his colleagues had a staff meeting at work on Friday morning, but I was out that night baking Christmas cookies with my mom, and Will went to visit Molly in Rockledge for the weekend. She'd asked him, in lieu of gifts this year, if he'd help her build some furniture, and he was more than willing. I love how close he is with his sister.

In any case, I'd totally forgotten to ask him about the staff meeting when he got home on Sunday afternoon.

Will smirks. "You seem awfully interested in this promotion. A guy could almost think you're just in this for the money."

"Will," I say sarcastically, "I think you're overestimating the salary of an interim library director."

He chuckles. "Perhaps. Nothing new came out of Friday's meeting, really. Lisa said the board is still planning to move forward with me in the role as long as I'm enrolled in my Master's program when the time comes."

"That's amazing!" I throw my arms around his neck excitedly. "I'm so happy for you!"

"Well, it's not a sure thing yet."

I offer him my sweetest smile. "What, are you planning to drop out of school again?"

He pretends to scowl. "Very funny. And anyway, I don't see how I can, when the woman I want to spend my life with is so invested in me chasing my dreams, and whatnot."

There's a moment, then, when we both look at each other, the realization of what he said about our future flashing between us. It's not a heavy feeling; instead, it hangs in the air like a cozy promise. I feel my cheeks flush.

"Well, it's the least I can do, considering how much you've done to encourage my writing pipe dreams."

Will shakes his head. "They're not pipe dreams."

"If it takes Jess much longer to sell either of my manuscripts, I'm really going to start to wonder."

"Callie, come on." Will surveys me thoughtfully. "It can take *years* to sell a book. Traditional publishing is not for the faint of heart."

He's right. I know he's right. But he believed in me so much right from the start that it made me think that I was really onto something with my writing. Like, even though it doesn't seem realistic, a publishing house would be tripping over its own feet to sign me. Like maybe there'd even be a bidding war.

I realize that's far-fetched. But, hey. A girl can dream.

"Well, perhaps I'll hear from Jess soon," I finally say.

Just then, my phone buzzes. I look down at the counter and see that it's a message from Jenna. *Did you end up booking at River's Edge?*

I pull my phone toward me and pretend to be closely studying the cake recipe. I hope Will didn't see the text. River's Edge is a B&B on the River Lee in Cork that Jenna highly recommended. She'd been there for her cousin's wedding a few years back and said it had the best scones on earth.

When I'm confident that Will is distracted, melting butter into the milk over the stovetop, I fire off a quick reply. *I did! Two nights there. I'm so excited!*

I can't wait to hear how he reacts! Text me tomorrow and let me know how it goes, she replies.

I don't usually delete my text messages, but I slide all three that Jenna and I just exchanged into the trash. Just in case.

It occurs to me that Will's not the only one keeping secrets today.

four

We bake for what feels like an entire lifetime, and then I'm about ready to collapse.

"Want to turn on the Christmas tree lights and just read for a while?" I suggest.

"That sounds amazing. I'm going to change real quick first." He indicates his shirt sheepishly. "I got a little flour on myself."

I chuckle at the white cloud superimposed on his black Rush concert tee. "You really did. Usually that's my jam."

"Save your jam for the Parker House rolls, Cal."

I can't help but roll my eyes. Will is so adorably corny.

I'm reading a book Susan lent me when Will pokes his head into the living room a few minutes later.

"I'm actually going to run an errand."

My confusion must show on my face. "An errand? But it's Christmas Eve."

He nods. "Yep. Stores'll be open for another few hours. I need to grab that champagne. And we forgot whipped cream, anyway."

"I'll just have my parents bring some over." I hop up and cross the room to Will, then throw my arms around his shoulders. "Please don't go. It's so cozy here."

Will kisses me deeply. "You drive a hard bargain."

"So stay," I plead, kissing him again.

He sighs. "I would, but I actually have another errand to run. Besides the groceries. I kind of have to."

"Ooh, intrigue." I tap his chest with my pointer finger. "Is this errand gift-related?" I figure if I can work my prying into the conversation organically, maybe it will be okay.

He grins mischievously. "Maybe."

My mind immediately flashes to the green wool coat I've been eyeing at Macy's. I'd tried it on the last time Will and I were at the mall, and it fit perfectly. It seemed like it would be perfect for our trip to Ireland in late March, but I couldn't tell him that, since the trip is a surprise.

Plus, I already have a winter jacket, a Columbia ski coat well-suited to our slushy mid-Atlantic winters. I thought buying another might raise suspicion. Still, I've been hoping that maybe I dropped enough hints, and he'll go back and get me the green coat for Christmas.

"Are you going...mall-ward?"

Will raises a brow in mock concern. "I thought you were a writer."

"Guilty."

"Pretty sure 'mall-ward' is not proper English." He grins. "But yes, I am headed in the general direction of the mall. Do you need anything?"

Yes, please. The green coat, the materialist in me wants to say. But I just smile and reply, "Just for you to hurry back."

"You're perfect, you know that?" He pulls me to him again, and we start making out in a way that I think even Scarlett would be disgusted by.

After a few minutes, I realize I need to let him go. We're watching *It's a Wonderful Life* tonight in honor of Esperanza (it was one of her favorites), and we have a special dinner planned—a taco bar and margaritas. We figure the salsa and guac are festive enough to make it holiday-appropriate.

The mall's going to be mobbed this afternoon, and I don't want Will to get tied up there. Not only will it suck for him, but it will also drastically cut into our movie time.

"Okay, get out of here," I say affectionately, giving him one last peck on the cheek. "I'll work on the cinnamon rolls while you're out."

"Perfect." Will grabs his coat and keys and heads out, while I move to the kitchen and dig around in the cabinet for the right cookbook.

My fingers hit a quartered piece of loose-leaf paper instead. Unfolding it, I see a recipe for ambrosia in Esperanza's handwriting. It's one of the few things she knew how to make, but she was always extremely proud of herself when she showed up to a party with it in hand.

Impulsively, I grab my phone and snap a quick picture of the recipe, then text it to Will. *Can you please grab these ingredients while you're out?*

It would make me feel very cozy indeed to prepare something Esperanza loved for Christmas this year.

Eventually, I locate the cookbook I'd been trying to find. It had slipped behind a mixing bowl and our food scale. The cinnamon roll recipe is flagged with a pink Post-it, because Will and I like having it easily referenced. We started making this treat for ourselves for breakfast on most holidays. It feels amazing to have our own traditions.

I've just turned on my Christmas playlist when my phone starts ringing. "Hey, Scarlett," I answer, gripping the phone between my shoulder and my ear while I stir together several dry ingredients.

"Oh my God, Callie. You're not going to believe what happened!"

I pause for a second. Typically, Scarlett's not really looking for you to actually say "What happened?" She just wants the briefest moment of dead air to make her feel polite enough that she can charge ahead.

Verily, she barrels on. "Jonathan's brother just flew in, totally unexpectedly."

I immediately see where she's headed, but I decide the inconvenience she's about to put me through means it's okay to make her work for this. "Oh?" I grin, alone in my kitchen, at the schadenfreude I'm perpetuating.

"Yeah. Josh was supposed to be in town on business next week, but his meeting got moved up to the 23rd. He figured he'd surprise us afterward, since he won't be here for Hanukkah."

"Well, that was nice of him," I reply.

"It was. Although the showing up unannounced at our house was slightly less appreciated, especially because we weren't exactly decent at the time."

It still strikes me as strange every time I hear her mention *their* house. Partially because it's a reminder that she and Jonathan are getting married in six months, and partially because it hits me all over again that she and I gave up our apartment almost a year ago, when Will and I moved in together.

Jonathan proposed to Scarlett last Thanksgiving, and when Will asked me if I wanted to find a new place together only a few weeks later, Scarlett and I decided it was probably time to let our apartment go.

Even though it's thrilling to be moving forward in life, and in love, it's still bittersweet sometimes to think about the life we left behind.

Also, leave it to Scarlett to insert casual mentions of her and Jonathan's extremely vibrant intimate life into every possible conversation.

"Anyway, so Josh is here, and we feel really uncomfortable leaving him alone tomorrow," she's rattling on. "Would it be okay if we brought him to your place? I promise I'll bring an extra appetizer to make up for it."

I snicker. "I was just making you sweat. Of course he's welcome here."

"You're hilarious," Scarlett remarks sarcastically.

I crack an egg into a bowl. "Believe me, I know."

"So, are you all set for Operation Emerald Isle?"

The oven beeps as I set it to temperature. Scarlett was the one who felt the need to coin a special phrase to describe my Christmas gift for Will. I explained to her several times that she should pick something more covert, so we could actually talk about it in front of him, but she apparently had her heart set on the least creative idea possible.

"Yep. Got the book and the tickets wrapped up earlier. He almost caught me in the act, but it's all good."

"Yikes!" she exclaims. "So, what do you think he's getting you?"

"I'm not sure," I say, rolling dough out onto wax paper. "There's a coat that caught my eye, and I think he knows about it. But otherwise, I don't really want anything. I'm pretty evolved these days, you know?"

"You're such a weirdo," Scarlett jokes. "Well, I should probably go. I need to finish wrapping Jonathan's Christmas gifts while he and Josh are busy playing Mario Kart."

"So he celebrates Christmas now?"

"Eh, not exactly," she admits. "I just want another excuse to spoil him, you know? Hanukkah feels so far away already."

"I love that you're so obsessed with him," I say, and I mean it.

"You and me both," she replies. "See you tomorrow, love!"

"Ciao!"

When I hang up from Scarlett, I text Will again. *Jonathan's bringing his brother tomorrow. We've never been so popular.*

He must be at the mall by now, because he shoots back: *Speak for yourself.* Then he sends a winky face.

I send another message to Susan, too, asking her to bring a third folding chair.

We might as well have this party at my house at this point, she jokes.

I snicker, but I realize she's at least a little bit right. The apartment is going to be bursting at the seams with guests tomorrow. I'm not certain we're going to have much extra room, but I think I'm okay with that. When I was a kid, our family parties were huge and boisterous and warm, and I find myself missing some of that cozy atmosphere these days.

After I pop the cinnamon rolls in the oven, I head back to my laptop. I've been working on a new book, and I figure I might as well get some writing done while Will's out.

I resist the urge to look at my email. It must be a Christmas miracle that I find the restraint. Instead, I pop open a Word document and get to work.

My new book is a romance, centering on a cute male historian and the woman who turns to him, desperate to find a long-lost relative. Part of me feels a little guilty, writing another story that draws so heavily on my personal experiences. Except, of course, in my case, the historian was a library clerk (Will) and the long-lost relative was actually the long-lost love of a relative (Johnny). But my real life has been especially compelling these last few years, and I often find myself marveling at how close to fiction my reality often seems.

I mean, consider what happened to Esperanza. The birthday dinner jump-scare, where we thought she'd been hit by a car. And then she actually was. How she almost walked away from such a horrific accident, and then didn't. The lost love, who just happened to be alive and well, pining after her.

These coincidences hardly seem real. And yet.

Maybe I'm just exceptionally adept at noticing the drama. Perhaps similar things happen to everyone, but maybe I pick up on it more readily because I'm always looking for a story. Because I have the mind of a writer, or something.

Alternatively, it could be Scarlett's fault. Being surrounded by someone so melodramatic for so many years is bound to have some sort of impact on a person. In fact, many of Scarlett's manuscripts have been cloying love stories where the couple is separated by circumstances. She's written several time-travel romances that ended in heartbreak. So it's possible I'm just particularly attuned to that sort of thing in the real world.

In a hilarious twist, Scarlett's latest book is actually a deeply disturbing thriller. She'd gotten so sick of her editors trampling her lake house romance to death that she'd scrapped that story entirely and fired her agent. Then, she'd started writing a dark, seriously unhinged novel about a woman who goes completely insane and starts stalking her high school boyfriend. She forces him to live in her shed, until one day, she has a psychotic break and kills him with a table saw.

Honestly, if I were Jonathan, I would be terrified.

I guess finding the love of her life was all it took for Scarlett to grow weary of romantic tropes. Now that she has the reality she wants, she can entertain the darker recesses of her mind in her writing.

It doesn't escape my attention that, as I've been allowing my thoughts to wander all over creation, I haven't actually gotten any writing done. I put some soothing holiday music on to try to divert my attention from musing about any number of things, then I dive back in.

five

Eventually, I do get into a groove with my story. It never ceases to amaze me how I can fall in love with new characters, despite how invested I get in those from previous manuscripts. Lilly told me once she thinks our characters are like our children—no matter how many kids you have, you're always going to love them all equally, just in different ways.

I write for over an hour before it hits me that Will should be home by now. Where did his errands take him? Typically, I try to avoid being a bundle of nerves when we're apart, but I do want to make sure everything's okay. It's started snowing again, and driving conditions might not be ideal.

I decide to give him a quick call and see what's up. Unfortunately for my anxiety, it goes straight to voicemail.

Even though I try to stay calm, my pulse feels awfully rapid when I massage a pressure point on my wrist. Will was acting pretty shifty earlier, and now he's not answering his phone. What the heck is going on?

Before I can call him again and let my EOE flag fly, I see a text pop up. But it isn't from Will. It's from Molly.

If she asks to bring another guest tomorrow, I'm going to lose my mind.

I take a deep breath and open her message.

So, small problem, it reads. *I hard-boiled the eggs for tomorrow before my shift yesterday. I like to let them cool a little before I peel them; it's easier. But then I went to work. And left the eggs on the counter. I think they might be spoiled now?*

Gee, Molly, do you *think?*

I pinch the bridge of my nose. It's already 4:30. Molly's working a 12 tonight and won't have time to make another batch of deviled eggs before the party tomorrow.

Don't worry about it, I text back. *We'll take care of the eggs.*

Thanks, Callie. You're the best.

I know it's silly, but my eyes fill with tears then. The perfect holiday I had envisioned is quickly devolving, and I feel powerless to stop it.

Having my grandparents around tomorrow is going to bring up all kinds of uncomfortable memories. Hosting Jonathan's brother, whom I've never met, will make the entire gathering feel much less personal, too. We could go without deviled eggs, but they're my dad's favorite, and I really wanted a third savory appetizer.

I can text Will again and ask him to get eggs, but if he's already swung by the store for the ambrosia ingredients, that will be yet one more delay in terms of his return home for our Christmas Eve together.

And where *is* Will, anyway? Maybe it's PTSD from Esperanza's accident, but I'm starting to get worried that not only is he not home, he's not texting me back. It's snowing, and most of the drivers on the road tonight probably have their minds on other things.

With a deep sigh, I decide to try him again. *Could you grab a dozen eggs on the way home?*

Who knows if he'll reply or not. At this point, I just hope he gets home safely.

I wander aimlessly around the apartment, looking for things to do and trying to calm myself down. First, I put my gift for Will under the Christmas tree, moving it around several times to find the optimal angle. Then, I fluff the pillows on the couch and set up two TV trays in front of it so we can eat during our movie later.

When five o'clock hits, I start cooking the ground beef for our tacos. I make them just the way Will likes, with plenty of smoked paprika and cilantro.

A half hour later, I chop lettuce, tomato, and onion and portion them out into small bowls on the kitchen island. At six, I sauté bell peppers in every color of the rainbow and set them next to the other vegetables.

I'm curious how long this food can sit out before we get botulism, but I figure we probably have a little while yet. I can always toss everything back into the refrigerator, but the peppers and beef would get cold. Reheating would definitely dry them out. Especially the peppers.

I'm starting to feel a little teary again, but I try to blink it away. *Will is safe, and there's a reasonable explanation for all of this*, I reassure myself. There has to be.

At 6:15, as I'm blending up a pitcher of margaritas, Will bursts through the door, bringing a gust of wind and some errant snowflakes along with him.

"I was so worried!" My frustration evaporates as I see him in the entryway, shaking off snow and trying to unwind his scarf. I run to him and wrap him in a tight embrace, knocking him off balance.

He catches himself on the wall. "I'm so sorry, Callie. I'm so, so sorry." Will buries his face in my hair, his signature affectionate move. It made my heart flutter the first time he did it, and not a thing has changed in the time since.

But I don't understand what took him so long, or why he wasn't answering my messages. I pull back a bit and peer into his eyes. "What happened?"

His gaze shifts downward. "I got held up," he says simply. "And then my phone died. I'm really sorry."

I'm hovering somewhere between worry, frustration, and just plain confusion. How could he have gotten held up? He was getting groceries and running one mysterious errand, which I'm almost certain had to be buying me that green coat. Why he left it for the last minute, I don't really understand. Even still, that should have taken him two hours, tops.

But he's looking at me like he's never seen anything more beautiful, and my stomach is growling in a big way, so I just grab his hand and pull him into the living room. "Dinner's ready," I announce, handing him a plate. "Let's start our movie."

I remind myself, once again, that Will usually does better if I let him come to me when he's ready to share. He must have a reasonable explanation for it all. And I'm sure he'll tell me, in time.

We get our food, clink our margarita glasses in a toast, and snuggle in to watch *It's a Wonderful Life*. At first, my mind is swirling with the tension of the day and the repeated last-minute additions to our guest list. I don't even bother to mention the missing appetizer to Will. Since his phone died, he never even saw my message about the eggs. Why add to his stress now?

But the tequila takes the edge off my frustration, and the anxiety of whether we'll be able to squeeze 15 people around Esperanza's table, which sits in a place of honor in our dining room, begins to dissipate. And when Jimmy Stewart cries at the beauty of his broken banister knob, I start crying, too.

I have a lot to be thankful for.

six

I wake up on Christmas morning to the sound of snow gently falling on the roof. Lifting the shade next to my side of the bed, I can see the flakes glistening as they swirl down out of the sky. It seems like an inch or two of fresh powder has dusted across the grass, but it shouldn't be so much that our guests are unable to get to us later.

Lifting the corner of my blanket as gingerly as possible, I creep out of bed and hurry to the kitchen. I need to grab the cinnamon rolls from the fridge and put them in the oven to warm them up.

When I open the refrigerator, two bottles of champagne clink on the door. I don't know how many mimosas Will thinks we're going to be consuming this morning, but I'm pretty sure we'll have plenty of leftover André.

Neatly laid across the top shelf are all of the ingredients for Esperanza's ambrosia. Will even managed to find the exact brand of maraschino cherries she specified in her recipe. My heart swells when I picture him, roaming the grocery store, carefully checking off each item on my list. I still have no idea what took him so long last night, but I'm not sure I care. I trust him, and he'll tell me when he's ready.

I slide the pan of cinnamon rolls into the oven on low heat and scramble back to bed. Will's still asleep, and it's only 8:30. We have plenty of time before we have to start getting ready, and there's very little I love more than spending a slow, cozy morning in bed.

After slipping back under the covers next to Will, I press myself against his body, craving both his warmth and the contact. He curls his arm over my waist and mumbles something that sounds like "I love you," but he's clearly not ready to be awake yet.

I start running through my task list for the day. I'm planning to set the table well ahead of time, as soon as I'm done vacuuming, since that might kick up dust. Then, I'll get all of our gifts for family and friends arranged under the tree and whip up the appetizers and sides we didn't make ahead: green salad, vegetables and dip, mashed potatoes. After that, I'll frost the cake I made yesterday and prep the ambrosia.

I wonder if seeing that all-too-familiar dessert on the table is going to make my mother cry. I'm also curious if I'll be able to stand there, reading Esperanza's recipe, without tearing up myself.

The last Christmas my whole family spent together, almost seven years ago now, Esperanza brought two things to my grandparents' house: her ambrosia and a fluffy Lisa Frank zip-up binder. She flew through the door in a whirlwind of nervous energy, set the dessert on top of a hot plate meant for the turkey, and immediately marched up to my father, brandishing the binder.

"Merry Christmas. Can you use this for your work?"

Everyone stopped talking, and I'm not sure I've ever seen my dad quite that taken aback. He finally managed a timid "N-no?"

And that was all it took to set Esperanza off.

For the next half hour, she mumbled to anyone who would listen about the sheer audacity of a person not wanting a child's Trapper Keeper covered in rainbow dolphins at their place of employment.

"I can't...I can't believe this. Once upon a time, everyone would have loved...everyone would have loved a leafler. Once upon a time."

At "leafler," Clare and I about lost it. I actually had to leave the room so that Esperanza wouldn't hear me laughing.

I never quite knew where to draw the line with her. Sometimes, it seemed like she enjoyed being the butt of lighthearted jokes, but at others, I thought maybe she was actually offended.

And, given how she was reacting to the rejection of her binder, I assumed that maybe this time was one of the latter.

She calmed down eventually and put herself to work, puttering around the kitchen and washing dishes that people weren't done with.

When we ate dinner, she helpfully offered to serve the turkey, which, for her, entailed walking up and down next to the table, holding out various grisly bird bits, and asking questions like, "Does anyone want the neck?" Shockingly, no one did, so she claimed it for herself.

After we opened gifts, she helped out by gathering up all the used wrapping paper and throwing it in the fireplace.

"That might have chemicals in it," I'd told her quietly. "You know, in the ink? We probably shouldn't burn it."

"It's just paper," she'd insisted. So I let it go, because she was already upset.

As it turned out, it wasn't just paper. She'd also burned several cards that contained cash gifts from my grandparents. They were none too pleased, but it was getting dark anyway, so she'd left in a huff and headed home.

I think that might have been the most insane holiday we ever shared together. It hurts, more than a little bit, to realize we're never going to have another one quite like that.

I'm wondering what ever happened to her "leafler" when Will starts to stir.

"Morning," he mumbles sleepily.

He looks so incredibly cute, hair all mussed against his pillow, that I lean down and kiss him on the cheek. "Merry Christmas, my love."

He grins and pulls me closer.

The apartment smells like baking cinnamon rolls, and I'm incredibly comfortable, wrapped up in Will and our flannel Lands' End sheets. They'd been a splurge from last Christmas, and they were worth every penny once the dead of winter hit.

In this moment, hearing the snowflakes fall on the roof, with the promise of a full house later on, and some vestiges of the magic of Christmas past humming through my veins, I think my heart might be about to grow three sizes. Not that I was starting at Grinch levels, or anything.

It occurs to me that once, not all that long ago, this scene was something I pictured. Almost note-for-note. Waking up to snow on Christmas; making love to Will in our very own apartment. The freshly baked cinnamon rolls for breakfast; opening our home to family later in the day. And now it's come true.

Well, nearly all of it.

And while I might be a dreamer, I'd also like to think I'm a go-getter. And the idea of a sexy Christmas morning is feeling pretty appealing at the moment.

So I decide to bring that dream full circle.

Will is fully awake now, smiling at me in the early morning light.

"Hey," I whisper against his cheek.

"Hey, yourself," he replies.

Tentatively, I lean forward and sweep my lips over his. It never ceases to amaze me how, even after all this time, kissing Will unleashes a lepidoptery lab's worth of butterflies in my chest.

He kisses me back, like being here with me means just as much to him as it does to me. Like I take his breath away, like he dreams about spending every Christmas morning for the rest of his life doing exactly this.

Then, I'm running one hand through his hair, the other over his bare chest, taking in the way he feels; the way he makes me feel. He wraps his arms around my back, skimming his fingers under the waistband of my pajama pants.

"Mmm," I murmur. "That feels nice."

"Oh, yeah?" he asks, in a way I can only think to describe as sultry.

"Yes. Very much so."

We lose ourselves in the moment again, matching caress for caress, kiss for kiss. My thoughts slip away in time with our breathing, growing increasingly rapid as we fall into the trance of loving each other.

When we stop to catch our breath, Will teases, "You know, I was hoping for a *certain* present this year." He tucks my hair behind my ear, lips still hovering just over mine.

I know he's joking, but I very much want to play along. "Well then, why don't you go ahead and unwrap it?" I'm pretty sure my eyes look just as inky as his do, pulled under by lust and love and the cozy warmth of this moment.

"Okay," he says, taking his time with my pajama shirt, undoing one button at a time. "But I should warn you—I'm not one of those guys who tears through a pile of presents in five minutes flat. I like to savor my gifts." He grins mischievously.

"Savor away," I say, kissing his neck.

And that's exactly what he does.

seven

When we're done crossing my perfect Christmas morning off my bucket list, it's almost 10:30.

"We have *got* to stop spending so much of our day in bed," I murmur into Will's chest.

He shakes his head. "Hard disagree. Let's do this every day."

I laugh loudly. "Okay, I've come around to your way of thinking. Consider it done."

"Do you want to grab the first shower?" he asks, drawing lazy circles along the curve of my hip.

"Yeah, I probably should. Although maybe it would make more sense to vacuum first, in case I get dusty?"

"I'll take care of that. You get cleaned up." His mouth quirks up on one side. "My Christmas gift to you."

I purse my lips. "You cleaning our apartment, which is half your job anyway, is your Christmas gift to me?"

"Well, one of." Will pretends to pout. "Did you not like the first gift I gave you?"

With all the solemnity of a silent night, I reply, "Best gift I've ever gotten. In fact, maybe you should join me in the shower so I can reciprocate."

He looks toward the door, which strikes me as odd, but not so odd as when he says, "It's okay. You go ahead. I'll get some of that cleaning done."

I've never known Will to turn down an offer for a joint shower, but I try to shrug it off. There *is* a lot we need to do before our guests arrive later. I guess it makes sense to bite the bullet and start getting ready now.

The water is hot, and my peppermint body wash smells divine. I spend perhaps 15 minutes longer than I should, luxuriating in the steam before stepping out onto the fluffy beige bath mat Will and I picked out together the day we signed our lease.

"We're going to need things. Towels. Pans. Bath mats," he'd said.

"Bath mats, plural?"

Will shrugged. "I don't know. Maybe. Let's go buy our first home good together to celebrate signing the lease."

And so we'd driven straight to the mall, picked the first bath mat we found in the Macy's housewares department, and left to go see a movie.

Thinking about Macy's makes me think about my green coat, which reminds me that Will still hasn't told me where he was last night. *Maybe after we open gifts*, I reassure myself.

When I push open the door to the bathroom, steam billowing out behind me, I catch a whiff of something—maybe candles? I can't imagine what Will's up to. I don't hear a vacuum, that's for sure.

After I get dressed in Will's Tom Petty shirt, a clean pair of pajama pants, and a fuzzy pink robe, I head out to the living room. And what I see takes my breath away.

The overhead lights are dimmed, and Will has candles lit on every available surface. Christmas music is playing softly in the background, and the tree is illuminated, its beautiful colors twinkling as they reflect off the ceiling.

Two steaming mugs of coffee are waiting for us in front of the couch, and I see three green-wrapped presents under the tree that weren't there last night when I went to bed. We don't have a fireplace, but Will has turned on a yule log video, so our TV looks like a crackling fire, set before it all.

It's pure magic.

He's leaning over Esperanza's ambrosia recipe at the counter, several cans of fruit set out next to him. "Hey." He looks up when he sees me. "I didn't actually start yet. I was just getting things ready."

"Thank you," I come to stand next to him and wrap him in a hug. "It looks beautiful out here," I breathe.

His smile is electric. "I'm glad you like it." Will straightens against the counter and grabs my hand. "Let's go open our presents before the coffee gets cold."

Sinking gratefully onto the couch, I pull a fleece blanket over my lap and take a sip of coffee. "Ahh. Perfect."

Will's stooping in front of the tree to gather the three gifts that I assume must be from him. He sets them next to me and settles in, expectantly.

"Hold on," I tell him. "Let me grab yours, too."

I'm feeling guilty that I only have one present for him to open, but I guess it *is* a pretty substantial gift. Maybe I should have wrapped the tickets and the book separately.

I shake off the thought. I'm pretty sure I could give Will nothing but a cookie and a hug, and he'd say he had the perfect day.

"Merry Christmas." I hand him the sparkly red package and kiss his cheek. "You go first."

Will raises an eyebrow. "You sure?"

"Absolutely." I don't think I can wait another second to spill the beans about Operation Emerald Isle.

Will's dark hair flops over his forehead as he bends over the gift, peeling back the tape. The book falls onto his lap.

"Whoa, cool!" He grins and picks it up, examining the front and back with reverence. "The Book of Kells is my favorite!"

"I know," I reply with a smile.

Will flips open the cover and stops when he notices the envelope lying atop the title page. He looks at me quizzically.

"Well, go on," I encourage.

He slides his thumb under the envelope flap and pulls out the plane tickets. "Ireland? Oh my God! Callie, this is awesome! How did you—"

I laugh, then, because how *did* I? It had felt like a Herculean task, at the time, arranging it all without him knowing. "It was a challenge," I admit. "But it was a lot of fun to plan."

"But what about work?" He looks concerned.

Shaking my head, I pat him on the shoulder. "Don't worry; I already cleared it with the library. And the trip is during spring break, so you won't miss any classes."

Will's looking at me with so much love in his eyes, I feel like my heart is going to overflow. "This is amazing."

The edge of my mouth tips up. "You'd better have one hell of a present in that pile for me if you're going to top a surprise trip to Ireland."

I'm joking, and I assumed he would know it, but he suddenly looks...nervous?

"I'm sorry," I correct quickly. "I was kidding. You could get me nothing at all, and the way you turned this room into the magical Christmas wonderland of my childhood would be gift enough for me."

He definitely set up the room this way on purpose. I've been waxing poetic about holidays of yore a lot lately, and it seems like he committed every detail to memory so he could recreate the aura here. Honestly, it's one of the sweetest things anyone's ever done for me.

"Open this one first," Will says, handing me the smallest box.

I tear open the paper to reveal a green leather-bound book. When I see the title, I gasp.

"Will, is this—"

He nods proudly. "First edition of *Gone with the Wind*. I found it at a shop up in Rockledge when I visited Molly last weekend."

My jaw drops. "Will, this is amazing. It's one of my favorites."

"Yes, I know," he teases. "That's why I got it for you."

I wrap him in a hug. "Thank you. I love it."

This is even better than the green coat.

"Ready for the next one?" Will gently nudges the second box toward me.

Whatever it is, it's inside a shoebox. "Am I going to find another box in here?" I joke.

His eyes twinkle. "Perhaps."

And, indeed, there is a smaller box inside the shoebox, and inside that is a copy of *Fault Lines*. I stare at it blankly for a moment.

"This is *your* book," I finally manage.

Will laughs out loud. "It's yours now. I just gave it to you."

I flip open the cover and see he's signed the title page. "To Callie, the love of my life."

"Wow, signed by the author!"

He puts his arm around my shoulder. "That one's a first edition, too."

I regard him mockingly. "I like how you had me open this *after* the 82-year-old copy of *Gone with the Wind*, as if to signify its relative value."

"Well," he shrugs, teasingly.

"You're ridiculous," I say, leaning over to kiss him.

"Guilty," he says against my lips.

We lose ourselves in each other for a few minutes. Then, he hands me the last present. It's a pretty large box. I'm wondering if this could be the coat.

Not that I really care all that much anymore. He's already given me so much.

"Thank you." I take the box and start to remove the wrapping paper.

Inside is a box from Macy's.

"I think I know where you went last night."

Will nods. "Do you, now?"

"Absolutely," I reply, pulling the lid off the box. Nestled in a bed of red tissue paper is the coat.

I remove it from the box gingerly, letting it cascade down to the ground. Its belt is tied in a bow at the front. "Oh my God, thank you! I really, really wanted this!" Because even though he's given me so much, and I would have been satisfied with no presents at all, the coat *is* beyond beautiful.

I throw my arms around Will, all the gifts forgotten beside me on the couch.

"Try it on." He looks nervous again.

I pat him on the head to reassure him. "Don't worry; I'm sure it will fit."

But I slip off my robe and put the coat on, then twirl around a little in front of the Christmas tree. This day is making me feel like a kid again.

"You look gorgeous," Will says. He's looking at me like I'm the brightest object in his universe.

"Aw, thanks. You make me feel that way."

I see a hint of a blush creep up his cheeks. "How's the belt? How are the pockets?"

I tighten the belt around my waist, then unbutton the pockets and slip my hands inside. "They seem good. Cozy. I think—"

I'm about to say, "I think this will be perfect for March in Ireland," when my fingers brush against something metallic in the left pocket. The room blurs a little in front of me as I take it out.

"Will," I breathe, holding up what must be the world's most perfect ring. It's rose gold, with an Art Deco design and several small diamonds set around the main stone. The diamond at the center is sparkling vibrantly, playing tag with the lights from the Christmas tree as they twinkle back and forth to each other.

He's in front of me now, wrapping me in his arms. My cheeks are wet, and I think his are, too. After a minute, he pulls back and draws me into the warmth of his smile.

"I'm in love with you. I think that's been true since the day we met. And I know it's never going to change for me." He tucks a stray strand of hair behind my ear, then gives me an adorable smile that makes my heart melt. "Callie, will you marry me?"

I'm nodding through tears, barely able to form words, thanks to the ecstatic feeling washing through my chest. "Yes. Yes, always. Forever."

He slides the ring onto my finger, and it fits perfectly, of course. I grab his face and pull him towards me and kiss him so deeply I think I'm transported to another planet. This is what I'm meant to do, I'm pretty sure—make Will happy and let him make me happy. This is why I was put here on Earth. I can't imagine ever wanting to be anywhere else.

All of a sudden, something acrid hits my nostrils. I pull back cautiously. "Um. What's that smell?"

Will's face turns horrified. "Oh, damn it!" He runs to the kitchen, pulling open the oven. I dash after him. Smoke billows out around the door, and I see my precious cinnamon rolls inside, looking like nondescript lumps of charcoal.

"Oops," he says meekly, turning to look at me.

"Oops," I return, and I start laughing at the absurdity of the situation.

Will runs his hand through his hair. "I'm so sorry. You spent so much time making those. I got...distracted, setting things up out here while you were in the shower. I should have taken the rolls out earlier."

I shrug and reach for him, momentarily distracted by the new sparkle on my left hand. "Frankly, I couldn't care one iota less." We kiss again. "And, anyway, chaos makes for a more interesting addition to our story."

"This is true," he muses. "All the best romances have a day where everything goes wrong."

"As long as I'm with you," I say, hooking his arm around my shoulders and grabbing the champagne whose importance I now understand, "there will never be a day where *everything* goes wrong."

eight

Will and I cuddle on the couch and toast each other over and over again. The day is gorgeous and languid and flowing, and I never want it to end.

But when two o'clock rolls around, we begrudgingly agree it's probably time to actually start getting ready for the 13 guests who are going to descend upon our home in just three hours.

"I'll make the ambrosia," I offer, jumping off the couch.

"I'll get started on the salad," Will says. "When I'm done, I'll clean the bathrooms and grab a shower."

"Break!" I say jokingly, like we're a football team.

We hurry about the apartment, rushing through tasks as if our lives depend on it, all to the soundtrack of the Christmas playlist on Will's phone. I feel like I'm in a movie montage.

We occasionally shout things to each other, like "Peeler?" or "Where's the Windex?", but otherwise we're focused on getting the apartment party-ready as quickly as possible.

When Will gets out of the shower, it's almost 4:30. If Esperanza were still alive, she'd already be banging down the door, like being fashionably early was the focal point of her identity.

A melancholy breeze whirls through me, but I try to brace

myself against it. Esperanza would be so, so happy today—for the holiday, for the turkey neck, to hear that Will and I are engaged. I'm going to pretend she knows. In some parallel universe, maybe she does know.

Will's damp hair is curling over his forehead, and he's put on a green-and-red plaid button-down that I bought him last Christmas. It was a bit of a joke, a reference to his love affair with Scottish fabric patterns. But my stomach lurches a bit when I see him in it now. The shirt hugs him in all the right ways, and he looks amazing, and goddamn it, I'm so incredibly happy right now.

"I love you." I practically leap into his arms.

"Jonathan warned me you'd get like this after I gave you expensive jewelry," he jokes.

I wrinkle my nose at him. "This is *not* because of the ring." I take in how it's glistening, even in the low light of the living room. "It does help, though."

He grins rakishly. "See? That's what I thought."

Something he just said hits me then. "Do Scarlett and Jonathan know already?" I hold up my hand.

Will nods. "Sort of? I needed the name of the jeweler Jonathan used. They did such an amazing job on Scarlett's ring."

"They really did." Scarlett's diamond, a 2-carat cushion-cut monstrosity, is surrounded by a halo of tiny rubies. It's quite possibly even more dramatic than she is.

"I didn't actually tell her, but I think Jonathan might have," Will says. "She started aggressively texting me Buzzfeed listicles with proposal ideas the next day."

I groan. Of course she did. "Oh, Scarlett."

Will laughs. "Oh, Scarlett."

"Wait." I must be a little slow on the uptake today. "This is a *custom* ring?"

Will's eyes are bright. "It is."

"Can we afford that?"

He squeezes my hand. "You're adorable. Actually," he runs his fingers through his hair. "I saved a lot of money by bringing my own diamond."

"You had a diamond hanging around here?"

"Well, technically, someone else had it."

I shoot him a quizzical glance. "I'm confused."

Will sinks onto the couch and pulls me down beside him. "The diamond was Esperanza's. At least, it was supposed to be."

My jaw drops. "She had a diamond? Or was supposed to?" I laugh a little. "Honestly, I'm still confused."

He chuckles, too. "I had a call from Carolyn about six months ago."

My brows wrinkle over my nose. "Johnny's daughter?"

Will nods. "Turns out, they've been going through his stuff, trying to rehome as much of it as possible."

"Is he okay?" Will had better not be about to tell me that Johnny's dying. I don't think I can handle that today.

"Oh, he's fine. They've just subscribed heavily to the idea of Swedish death cleaning."

I snort. "So they're basically just decluttering?"

"More or less. He doesn't want Carolyn to have to deal with things when he's gone." Will grabs my hand. "Anyway, he had a ring."

The reality of what he's saying is starting to sink in. "He was going to propose to Esperanza?"

Will nods. "He was. That day, when Josephine came to the door."

Just like in my book. But I had no idea it was true when I wrote it. I was just following the story to what I thought was its logical conclusion.

Grief hits me like a wave. Not the kind that you splash through on the edge of the shore. The kind that comes up behind you while you're bobbing up and down on a peaceful beach day and knocks you over, filling your nose with salt water that stings.

My eyes are wet. "Johnny kept it all this time?"

"Carolyn said he came back from Esperanza's parents' house that day and put it in a drawer. He kept hoping he'd get a chance to propose. But then he shipped out, and evidently, he couldn't ever bring himself to sell it."

"But what about his first wife? I can't imagine she was very happy about him keeping an engagement ring he bought for someone else."

"I don't think she knew," Will replies. "Apparently she wanted to wear her own grandmother's ring, so Johnny never had to buy a second one. I guess Esperanza's just lived in a corner of his drawer all that time."

I shake my head. "That's pretty incredible."

"Right?" Will looks like he still can't quite believe it himself. "Carolyn said she was sorry if it was too personal, but that Johnny wanted me to have the ring. For you, if I planned to...well, you know." He smiles sweetly. "And I had already been planning to propose. So it all aligned really perfectly."

"Did they just give it to you for free?" This is quite the thing to just hand off to someone.

"I tried to pay them. They wouldn't take anything." His mouth curves up. "They might or might not be getting a very large fruit basket from us for Christmas, though."

I snort. "Well, that was very generous of us." I tip my fingers up so the ring catches the light again. "So, what did Esperanza's ring look like?"

"Just a silver band with the diamond," Will replies. "Pretty basic, but very elegant."

I swallow hard. "She would have loved it."

He wraps his arm around me, and I lean in to the warmth of his chest. "She would love that you have it."

And I know he's right.

"I'll have to call Johnny sometime," I say finally. "To thank him, and Carolyn. This is quite possibly the best Christmas present I've ever received, and I appreciate their part in it."

"Excuse you?" Will's eyes are twinkling. "You like this more than my book?"

"More than the book that you pulled out of a box of author copies that we keep in our closet?"

"Hey, I signed it just for you. And nestled it in not just one, but *two* boxes."

I snort. "Okay, I like that gift, which was clearly meant to be a joke, and my stunning engagement ring the same amount. Does that make you happy?"

"So very much." Will rubs his thumb across the back of my hand. "Hey, I wanted to apologize for last night. I'm assuming I worried you when I didn't answer your messages."

I'm glad he's bringing it up so I don't have to ask. "I actually called you, also. But if your phone was dead, that probably didn't even show up once you got it charged."

He shakes his head. "Nope. I should probably start carrying an extra charger in my car."

"So, where all did you have to go last night?" I ask. Now that the secrets are out, I figure it's okay to pry.

"Well, I had to order your coat ship-to-store," he explains. "They didn't have your size in stock. It was supposed to come in late last week, but when I went to pick it up, the one they sent was missing a button. So they ordered it a second time."

"I feel guilty that you put in so much effort on my behalf."

He chuckles. "Why? I think you might be more in love with that coat than you are with me."

"Never," I promise him, shaking my head passionately. "I do really like it, though."

"As well you should," he replies. "It really suits you."

"Aw, thanks." I get lost in his eyes for a minute, then take a deep breath. "So, what was that phone call about?"

He looks puzzled for a minute, then realization hits. "Oh. You saw that?"

"Well, I had to go over by the sink, and I noticed you outside.

And besides," I say with a tilt of my lips, "it normally doesn't take you ten minutes to check the mail."

"Guess I need to work on my sneaky behavior, then."

"Alternatively, you could stop keeping secrets," I tease.

"Secrets, secrets are no fun, for sure." Will cracks a smile. "This was about your ring, though. The jeweler was making some last-minute adjustments, and they left a voicemail yesterday saying it wouldn't be ready until after the holidays. But I had been planning to propose to you on Christmas for ages. Ever since you started talking about reclaiming the magic of the season, and whatnot."

"Oh," I reply. "It looked like you were really giving them hell on the phone."

He shrugs. "I mean, it wasn't the *most* polite I've ever been. But, to be fair, this was supposed to be done weeks ago. They kept pushing it back, and I was pretty upset."

I snort. "Seems like it paid off, at least."

"They called me back a while later, while you were reading on the couch, to say that they were all set. Funny how they suddenly managed to find time in their day that they'd previously claimed didn't exist."

"Isn't that always the way?"

"Anyway," he continues, "After I went to get the coat, I had to pick up the ring. Naturally, the place was mobbed when I went in." He smiles ruefully. "Lots of husbands buying their wives last-minute jewelry because they didn't bother to plan ahead."

"Promise you'll never buy me last-minute jewelry?" I meet his gaze.

"Scout's honor," Will says, trying not to laugh. "All of my last-minute gifts will always just be things we already have around the house, pulled out of the closet and hurriedly wrapped when you aren't paying attention."

"Like your book?"

"Precisely," he says, kissing my hair.

"I can't wait to be married to you." I cuddle into Will's chest.

"You and me both," he replies.

nine

As it turns out, the first guests to arrive that evening are Scarlett, Jonathan, and Josh. Scarlett's eyes immediately jump to my hand.

"Ahhhh! I knew it!!!" She attacks me with a hug that almost knocks me over. "Congratulations, you two!!!!"

Will is blushing pretty intensely, simultaneously accepting both one arm of Scarlett's enormous hug and a handshake from Jonathan.

A tall, gangly guy in a blue polo shirt and khakis who looks very much like Jonathan is standing awkwardly in the entryway. I manage to free myself from Scarlett's embrace.

"You must be Josh." I stick out my hand. "Nice to meet you; I'm Callie."

Josh nods politely. "It's a pleasure. Thank you so much for having me today. And congratulations!" He indicates my ring.

"Josh brought eggnog cake," Scarlett says, pointing to the frosted Bundt in his hand. "And here's the spinach dip, and our bonus, conciliatory appetizer, deviled eggs."

So I guess my dad will get his favorite snack after all.

"You guys are the best," I reply gratefully, taking the dish from Josh and gesturing to Scarlett to bring the others into the kitchen.

As soon as we're out of earshot, Scarlett grabs my hand and squeals. "Show me your ring!"

I suppose I'm going to have to get used to this; everyone else who shows up tonight is probably going to do the same thing. I let her twist and turn my wrist in every conceivable direction so she can see the diamond sparkle in the track lighting gleaming down from above us.

"So how did he do it?" Her eyes are intent on my face. "Tell. Me. Everything!"

I chuckle at her intensity, which never seems to fade. "Why, are you eager to find out if Will used one of the ideas from your Buzzfeed articles?"

She wrinkles her nose at me. "He told you about that?"

I nod, feigning concern. "He said you were beyond obsessed with sending him proposal ideas. To the point that it was unhealthy."

Scarlett sticks her tongue out at me. "None of that sounds like something your fiancé would say."

The word ignites something in my chest. Will and I have only been engaged for a few hours, but it's the first time I've heard someone call him my fiancé. I must say, I'm pleased with the upgrade.

"He just did it here," I explain, gesturing to the living room. "Candles, Christmas tree all lit up. He hid the ring in the pocket of that green coat I wanted." I take a deep breath, remembering how perfect the moment was. "It was somehow totally unexpected, and yet it was exactly what I've always wanted. It was so *us*, you know?"

Scarlett nods sagely. "Absolutely."

Jonathan had proposed to Scarlett during their Thanksgiving beach vacation last year, with shells on the sand spelling out "Will You Marry Me" and a local band serenading her as he got down on one knee. There had been a photographer to capture every second of the proposal, and Jonathan flew their families down for a celebratory weekend immediately afterward.

And that kind of public, dramatic proposal was exactly right for

Scarlett. But this one, here, in our home, filled with sentiment? This was just right for me.

The doorbell rings then. Will, still talking near the entryway with Jonathan and Josh, lets Molly in and introduces her to the newcomer. I think I catch Josh doing a double-take when he sees Molly's red sheath dress. I give Scarlett a knowing look, which she reciprocates. Maybe there will be more holiday magic being made here than we'd bargained for.

Susan and her family arrive in a cloud of well-meaning chaos a few minutes later, and the party really gets underway. I give each kid one of their gifts to try to keep them occupied so the adults have a shot at carrying on a conversation for a few minutes. They unceremoniously tear off the wrapping paper in about ten seconds, and then they're on their parents immediately, demanding help with inserting batteries and reading instructions.

Oh well. At least I tried.

When my mom and dad troop in with my grandparents in tow, we pull out the second bottle of champagne. Molly and Josh have retreated to a corner of our living room to talk, and I don't think Molly, or Susan or Doug, has noticed my ring. There's been too much going on.

"Callie and I have an announcement to make," says Will during a lull in the cheerful chatter.

My mom's eyes shoot towards me, and my father gives me a knowing glance. Josephine smiles quietly, and my grandfather continues standing stoically in the kitchen, reading the nutrition facts on a bottle of soda.

"As it turns out," Will continues, "I can't live without Callie. So, this morning, I asked her to marry me, and she said yes."

Susan gasps, and my mom's hands fly to her mouth in excitement. The room fills with cheers and clapping as everyone runs to wrap us in hugs and congratulations. My hand has never been so popular. Everything about the moment is perfect.

Scarlett pops open the champagne and starts handing it out in flutes to our assembled guests. "A toast to Callie and Will!" she shouts, raising her own glass in the air and sloshing some of it onto Jonathan's pants. "Sorry, babe," she says, dabbing at the spill with a paper towel.

When everyone toasts "To Callie and Will," I blink my eyes hard, like I'm taking a picture, like I can freeze this memory in time. I know I'm going to want to come back here someday.

ten

Dinner is bright and chaotic and loud. We end up with eight people crowded around Esperanza's table, five at TV trays in the living room, and Molly and Josh balancing plates precariously on their legs, sitting on the couch.

The food is delicious (she remarks humbly), and we stuff ourselves silly. My mom wants to hear all about Will's proposal, and she interrupts me about six hundred times to gush over my ring.

Scarlett talks Susan's ear off for 45 minutes about wedding planning, and Doug and my dad have a spirited conversation about referees of the NFL. My grandparents sit quietly at the table, saying very little, but smiling politely whenever they're addressed. I get the sense they're a little uncomfortable here.

After we eat, my grandmother finds me loading the dishwasher. "I'm so happy for you and William," she tells me.

"Thanks," I say, feeling the air around us ripple with the veil of formality we've been hiding under since Esperanza died.

"You know who else would be happy for you?" She steps forward like she wants to touch me, but stops herself.

I incline my head and force a smile. "I think I do."

"Can I see your ring?" She's so hesitant; so afraid. I think she really meant it that day after the funeral—she believes she's a horrible grandmother.

She hasn't been the best, it's true. But I know she's trying. And Esperanza would want me to try harder, too.

So I try.

I hold out my hand to her, my fingers shaking a little. "It was Esperanza's diamond," I say quietly.

Something like shock washes over her face. "Esperanza's?"

I nod quickly. "From Johnny."

"Oh." Josephine blinks rapidly. "I see."

She probably has no idea that Johnny bought a ring. Yes, she sent him packing the day he came by to ask Esperanza to wait for him, shortly before his Army unit was shipped abroad.

And she knew Will had come looking for Johnny's address right before Esperanza died.

But for all she knows, that was it. I never told her that Will and I met Johnny and his daughter, or that Johnny said he'd never moved on. I certainly never let on that I still talk to Johnny once a month or so on the phone.

I had the sense that sharing any of this with my grandmother would just make her feel even worse about the role she played in what happened. About how she diverted the course of two people's lives so they would never meet again.

She's certainly not perfect, but I think that knowledge could break just about anybody. And I'm worried that the look on her face right now means the full scope of what she did is starting to sink in.

I want to fix this, to make everything feel okay again. So even though I'd rather head back to the living room and talk to someone else, I tell her the story of how Will came to have the diamond.

I make it seem bright, and optimistic, and spirited, like Esperanza would have done. I tell her about the proposal, how beautiful it was. How Will made everything perfect.

I tell her about my green coat, and the books Will bought me. Our trip to Ireland, and Will's opportunity at the library. I want her to understand that, not only am I working hard to forgive her, but that she means enough to me to share the things that matter. Both the big things and the everyday.

And when I'm done, I put my arm on her stooped shoulders and say, "Can I show you some ornaments Will and I made?" And we walk together to the Christmas tree, where I tell her about the clay version of *Fault Lines* and the seashells and the red bulb ornaments we painted with fabric paint one night while watching *How the Grinch Stole Christmas*.

I don't know what it's going to feel like later, or even tomorrow, once the magic of the holidays starts to dissipate and reality begins to set in again.

But for right now, things are feeling like they just might be okay.

At 7:30, we pull out the dessert, and Will's phone dies. "Playing Christmas music uses a lot of battery life," he says.

"You are *really* not having great luck with your phone," I remark. "Is that what you were doing in the car yesterday that made the battery die? Listening to too much Mariah Carey?"

"Ew, never." He shakes his head vehemently.

"Mannheim Steamroller?" I try again.

He covers his eyes in mock embarrassment. "Okay, you got me."

I laugh. "Want me to plug in your phone? We can use my laptop to play the nerdy Christmas music."

"Sure, you can put on your playlist," he jokes, purposely misunderstanding my dig at his musical preferences. I pretend I'm about to playfully slap him, but I swoop in to kiss his cheek instead.

Will surveys me with mock concern. "You know, just because we're engaged doesn't mean you have to start fetching things for me."

I roll my eyes. "Believe me, that isn't a thing I'll be doing."

His laughter echoes in my chest as I walk into our bedroom.

I plug Will's phone into the power strip under his nightstand. Then, I cross to my desk and turn on my laptop.

From the living room, I hear Scarlett loudly cackling at something Doug has said, and Josh telling Molly about his job. They're still canoodling on the couch. I'm wondering if we've started something tonight with the two of them. My parents are talking in low voices with Josephine about whether the snow outside is going to make it hard to drive home. I'm pretty sure my grandfather's snoring.

When my computer boots up, I can see I have five new emails. Five new shards of optimism, twinkling in the ether, and ready to slice my confidence when they come crashing down.

Before I can think better of it, I open my inbox. Amazon, Lands' End, holiday greetings from our landlord. Spam, and—something from yesterday at 3:15 in the afternoon. Something from Jess.

I click it open greedily. And then my jaw falls open. My life is about to change.

eleven

Susan and Doug gather their brood at eight. "You can have chocolate from your stocking when we get home," Susan bribes a wailing Freya.

"But I want to stay and play with Callie and my typewriter!"

I will my face to remain a blank slate so as not to make this harder on Susan, but inside, I'm beaming like a July sun. I *knew* Freya was going to love her typewriter.

"How about I come over and play with it at your house sometime?" I ask, kneeling down to Freya's level.

She nods raggedly, sniffing back tears. "O-o-okay. Thank you!" Freya jumps into my arms, her little hands wrapping around my neck in a way that makes my heart melt.

"I love her," I whisper to Susan.

She flashes me a huge grin.

My parents leave about a half hour later, citing a need to get my grandparents to bed.

"If I stay up much later, I'll miss the morning financial report," my grandfather mutters to himself as they hug their way out the door.

"Anyone want to play charades?" Scarlett asks once it's just her group, Molly, Will, and me.

"You just want to play a game you can win," I tease her, thinking about how she crushed us every single time we played charades that weekend at Lake Manacqua. There must be something to having an overly theatrical personality that helps you win games like this.

"Damn straight I do. Like you aren't the same way."

"Right?" Will chimes in. "With Scattergories!"

I look between the two of them in mock fury. "Okay, I don't need you two ganging up on me."

They both laugh.

It occurs to me we still have two cartons of eggnog and a liter of rum that we'd bought for the party. "Can I fetch anyone a spiked eggnog?"

Everyone but Jonathan accepts, since he's planning to drive home later. Scarlett, forever the passenger, asks for extra rum. When I turn to walk back to the kitchen, I notice that Molly's hand is inching dangerously close to Josh's leg.

"Is Molly staying here tonight?" I whisper to Will, who's joined me in the kitchen to help with the drinks.

"She'd talked about it," he says. "Although, given the state of things in the living room, it's also possible she's going home with Josh."

I snicker. "I caught that also."

"I don't know how I'd feel about having my sister and Scarlett be sisters-in-law," Will jokes.

"We could all be one big, happy, boisterous family." I grin, because I'm kidding, but then I keep smiling, because it actually sounds like a really cozy thing that only happens in books. And I kind of want it to happen in our real lives, too.

We return to the living room with a tray full of eggnogs, plus a seltzer for Jonathan. Scarlett has already divided us into teams. Her group, which, naturally, got to go first, is giving its first clue.

"This is like that scene in *The Muppet Christmas Carol*," I say in Will's ear as I settle back against him on the couch. When Fred and Clara and an assortment of Victorian Muppets play party games.

Hopefully, Michael Caine's Scrooge isn't watching from the outskirts of our living room.

"You might just be the world's biggest nerd," he says.

"I'm sorry to have usurped your title," I smirk.

He squeezes my arm. "I forgive you."

"Unrelated, but I have another surprise for you. Later, once everyone's gone." I'm trying to keep my face even, but a never-ending smile is breaking through despite my best efforts.

"Oh?" He raises an eyebrow with great interest.

I shake my head. "Not that kind of surprise."

"Bummer."

"Well, maybe that kind of surprise. But something else, too."

Will grins. "I look forward to it."

twelve

As it turns out, Molly is not staying with us. She's had too much to drink to get home safely, but Scarlett offers they can take her back to their house.

"I don't want you to have a houseguest the night of your engagement," she smirks at me.

I start to stick my tongue out at her, but I realize I really would prefer some alone time with Will tonight. And it has nothing to do with what Scarlett's implying. It's just been a long day—a long couple of days, really. I want some time to just *be*, together.

Not to mention, I still have my exciting news to share with him.

Scarlett turns to Molly. "We live close by. "I'll bring you back in the morning so you can grab your car."

Molly's eyes light up, and she looks directly at Josh, who seems beyond thrilled that, for him, the festivities might not be over.

"Let me help you get your coat," he offers to Molly before hustling off to fetch it for her.

Scarlett raises an amused eyebrow, then comes to give me a good-night hug. "We agree this is going to be a thing, right?"

"Oh, 100%," I say back. "I'm glad you're perpetuating it."

She laughs loudly. "It's what I do."

I give her a tight squeeze. "Thanks for coming, Scarlett. And for bringing all that food."

"And for taking all *this* food," Will adds, thrusting five recycled takeout containers packed with leftovers at her.

She starts to protest, but I cut her off. "You have two guests tonight. You'll be all set if anyone gets the midnight munchies."

It takes another 20 minutes before Scarlett, Jonathan, Josh, and Molly finally make their way out the door. Everyone's too chatty, and, aside from Jonathan, too tipsy, to put an end to the merriment.

When the jingle bell on our front door finally goes quiet, Will sinks back against the kitchen counter with a deep sigh.

"What a day," he remarks, looking about as exhausted as I feel.

I cross the room to him and put my arms around his waist. "It was a great one, though."

"I know what could make it even better." He tips his head toward me. "Want to watch *The Muppet Christmas Carol?*"

"Aw, Will." I squeeze his hand. "I thought you'd never ask."

"But first," he says. "You had something to tell me?"

I nod, suddenly unsure I can deliver this news without grinning maniacally like the Joker. There's just been so much emotion to the holiday already—from the unexpected guests to the missing appetizers to Will's mysterious behavior to the engagement. And it all has turned out more than okay, but I feel like I'm positively overflowing with *feeling.*

I guess I got what I wanted out of Christmas after all.

"So, when I went to plug in your phone earlier," I begin, "and grabbed my laptop, I happened to notice an email. From yesterday." I take a deep breath. "From Jess."

Both of Will's eyebrows shoot up his forehead. "From Jess?"

"Mmhmm."

His grin is so bright, I think it could power an entire city's worth of Christmas lights. "Are you saying what I think you're saying?"

My heart is pounding in my chest in the best possible way, and I feel tears start behind my eyelids, even though I really thought I'd be able to make it through this without crying.

I nod, wiping my eyes with the side of my hand. "She had a meeting this week and was waiting to tell me until she knew for sure, but...she sold both books. They're getting published. I'm going to be a published author."

Will clearly doesn't know what to do with his excitement. We're both at that point, emotionally, where the feelings don't have anywhere to go. If we were kids, I think we'd probably be jumping up and down and screaming.

"Oh my God, Callie!" He wraps me in the tightest hug imaginable. "I am so, so happy for you! Oh my God! This is amazing!"

"I know! I can't even believe it!" I feel saltwater against my lips, which are shaking, I'm grinning so much. "I just...I never thought all of my dreams would come true in one day, you know?"

Will kisses the top of my head. "If anyone deserves that, it's you." He pulls back and gives me a quizzical look. "Why didn't you break the news to everyone while they were here earlier?"

I shrug. "I really wanted you to know first. Honestly, I'm not sure I'd be here without you."

His eyes twinkle. "That's categorically true, since this is *our* apartment. I think you'd still be in your old place with Scarlett without—"

"No, you weirdo. I mean here, in a more metaphorical sense. A soon-to-be-published author."

"Well," Will straightens up self-importantly, "I *was* your first beta reader. And I do have that whole riding-your-coattails-all-the-way-to-a-Pulitzer thing that I committed to." He takes my hand. "But there's plenty of time for that. Now, I think it's time to watch Michael Caine give an Oscar-level performance across from a bunch of marionette-puppet hybrids."

My smile goes all the way to my eyes. "I think that sounds perfect."

We cuddle on the couch and eat leftover ambrosia straight out of the bowl. Esperanza's diamond sparkles in the light of the Christmas tree, and Will's arm is warm around my shoulders. Snow is falling softly outside our window, and Ireland will be green in the spring. The house smells like cinnamon and pine, and my heart is full.

And when the Ghost of Christmas Present tells Scrooge that anywhere there's love, it feels like Christmas, it hits me that truer words have never been written.

It's surreal to be writing my second author's note in one year. In what felt like a blink, I went from always wanting to be an author to having both a published novel and this novella, with another novel on the way. To say this is a dream come true would be an understatement.

I've been overwhelmed by the love for Callie, Will, and Esperanza since *Ghost Writing* was released. Your kind words have meant so much to me as a debut author, and I will be forever grateful that you've taken this journey with me. I am even more blown away that I've been given the opportunity to return to Callie and Will's story here, in *Ghosts of Christmas Presents*. It's such an incredible joy to write these characters, and I hope to be back someday. (Stay tuned for books set in the *Ghost Writing* universe about Scarlett and Jonathan and Molly and Josh!)

If you've read *Ghost Writing*, you know that Esperanza is based on someone who was incredibly special to me, and the fact that her story led me to Callie and Will is just another in a laundry list of things that I will always cherish about her.

I can't emphasize enough how I didn't expect my life to bring me to this place. For more than eight years, I've worked as a self-employed marketing writer, and before that, I worked in publishing.

For most of my career, I've been surrounded by words and stories, always dancing around the idea of fiction writing but never quite believing I could cross that line myself.

The sad thing is, I've wanted to be a writer since I was a child. I've found countless ways to get really close—but imposter syndrome has always held me back.

Ghost Writing started as a quiet "what if." What if I actually tried? What if I wrote something that wasn't for a client or a campaign, but for me? And for Esperanza?

Somehow that "what if" turned into a whole novel and then this novella — books that are now out in the world, finding readers. And honestly, that still feels a little unbelievable.

While the Callie and Will storyline in my books isn't directly based on my life, there's a lot of me in Callie. She's a ghostwriter, like me, and she also struggles with self-limiting thoughts. If you've walked any part of this journey yourself, or have ever dreamed of becoming more, you might see yourself reflected in her, too.

I'm here to remind you that your brain is lying to you. You may not succeed in everything you do, but you CAN try. You owe it to yourself to live authentically. I promise, the feeling of relief from knowing you're following the path that feels like it was made just for you is worth every bit of effort.

So, thank you for reading. Thank you for allowing me to pursue this dream. And, since you're here, I would ask you to take a moment to reflect—what unfulfilled dreams do *you* have? If you take anything away from my books, let it be this: there is nothing quite like living authentically and pursuing the paths that feel right to you, deep down. I wish you the best of luck on your journey.

Danielle Smyth

Danielle Smyth has dreamed of being a writer since childhood, and seeing that dream realized is the ultimate happy ending. When she's not writing, Danielle runs a small business. Her favorite days are spent traveling, eating tacos, and reading with her family.

also by danielle smyth

Ghost Writing

www.ingramcontent.com/pod-product-compliance
Lightning Source LLC
Chambersburg PA
CBHW071135100726
47908CB00008B/2609